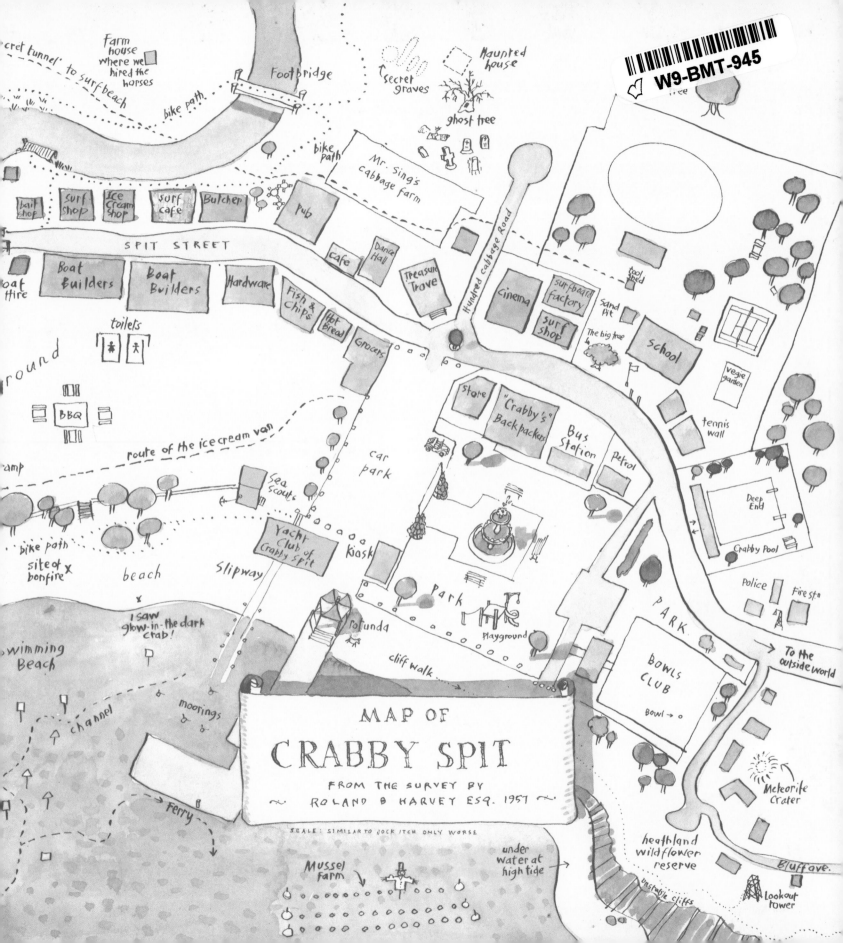

W9-BMT-945

'Secret tunnel' to surf beach
Farm house where we hired the horses
Footbridge
bike path
secret graves
Haunted house
ghost tree
bike path
Mr. Sing's cabbage farm

bait shop
surf shop
Ice Cream shop
surf cafe
Butcher
pub
Hundred cabbage Road

SPIT STREET
Cafe
Dance Hall
Treasure Trove
Cinema
surfboard factory
surf shop
tool shed
sand pit
The big tree
School
vegie garden
tennis wall

Boat hire
Boat Builders
Boat Builders
Hardware
Fish & Chips
Hot Bread
Grocers
toilets
ground
BBQ
route of the ice cream van
ramp
Sea Scouts
car park
Store
"Crabby's" Backpackers
Bus Station
Petrol
Deep End
Crabby Pool

bike path
site of bonfire X
beach
Slipway
Yacht Club of Crabby Spit
Kiosk
Park
Playground
tennis wall
Police
Fire Stn

I saw glow-in-the-dark crab!
rotunda
cliff walk
PARK
BOWLS CLUB
Bowl →
To the outside world

swimming Beach
channel
moorings
Ferry

MAP OF
CRABBY SPIT
FROM THE SURVEY BY
ROLAND B HARVEY ESQ. 1957

SCALE: SIMILAR TO JOCK ITCH ONLY WORSE

Mussel Farm
under water at high tide
heathland wildflower reserve
Bluff ave.
unstable cliffs
Meteorite Crater
Lookout tower

For Frankie

Goodbye, my darlings! Don't forget to write!

Rajah

Frankie

At the BEACH

Postcards from Crabby Spit

Roland Harvey

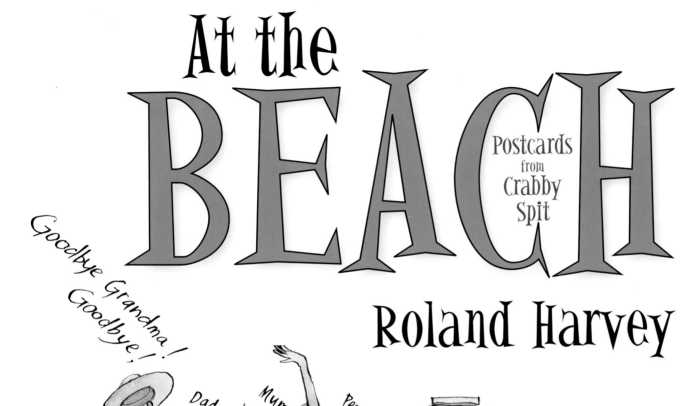

Goodbye Grandma! Goodbye!!

Dad

Mum

Penny

Henry

Pierre

ALLEN&UNWIN

Welcome to
CRABBY SPIT

MR-CRABBY

Dear Grandma
We are nearly at Crabby Spit! On the way we had
to stop 3 times and Frankie was sick 4 times. We saw
a policeman and he told dad to speed up because he
was holding up traffic.
We saw a monster in a lake and I saw 12 baby ducks
and 2 giant crabs.
Rajah found a towel beside the road! I can't wait
to get to Crabby Spit. I drew us for you. Love from
Henry

Dad   Mum   Penny   Frankie
Rajah

Dear Grandma, Crabby Spit is <u>COOL</u>!
We have the best camping spot right near the
toilets and the beach and the river. Mum has
agreed to stop embarrassing us and only wear her
new hat in the tent if we do <u>ALL</u> the cooking for
the <u>whole</u> holiday. One family has brought their
mower and we are getting fish and chips for tea
and then going looking for crabs. There is a bike
track and a river and horse riding and mosquitoes.

Love from Henry

Dear Grandma ... Wow!! It's all happening at Crabby. Dad says the lifesavers are wanting him to join the club and Mr. Mac Intosh was chased by a shark. It must have been scared off by the taste of his shorts. And I saw a bird drop a poo on a kid's hand. I'm going to join the lifesavers and row the surfboat and drive the rubber duckies. I tell you what, Grandma, surfing is ace. I am going to get really good and be world champ. There was a hang-gliderer and I want to be worldchamp of that too. That's after I get to be world champignon at Frisbee. I drew this picture of a hang-gliderer for you!
♡ love ♡ Penny

Dear Grandma, We are having a good time here at Crabby Spit. At the Sand Sculpture Competition today Mrs. Thomas made Mr. Thomas into a mermaid and won! The kids helped dad build a sandcastle and Uncle Kevin is going to have another go at the surfboard. One kid thinks he is a seagull and a little dog did a wee on a lady's foot. Some people have been catching fish and they showed us how to clean them. I have become a vegetarian. I don't know how the seagull kid does it. He only stays up for about 20 seconds so I think he's cheating.

♡ Penny

Hey Grandma! I couldn't find a pen so I had to use a stick dipped in paint. It is really pouring today so we went to Treasure Trove and bought some cool stuff. I wanted some 20m white pointer jaws but got a snake instead. Mum bought dad an ironing board because he thinks he's Iron Man.

See ya, Henry

Dear Grandma, I bet you would <u>love</u> Crabby Spit. It is so windy today that I saw some underpants fly across the camping ground. The last I saw they were on the back of a lady's head.

We played Scrabble in the annexe and had hot chocolate and marshmallow floaters. Afterwards we helped clean up the beach. Mr Thomas' stuff floated away yesterday and today the wind is blowing it all back again! Dad is going to buy a heap of fish and chips and invite everyone to a party!

I hope Frankie's mice and my axolotl are OK and not too much trouble.

♡ from Penny

DEAR GRANDMA

Mum is helping me write this postcard because she is very sunburnt and has to stay in the shade.
Uncle Pete and Auntie Sam came to visit and we beat them at beach cricket. Penny bowled Uncle Pete for a duck and I saw a snake. And I missed a catch because I was busy surfing.
Mum is teaching me to swim and I can put my face in the water right up to my chin.
Dad is cooking his big fish tonight!
bye FRANKIE

Dear Grandma

We have been floating down the river and doing bombs off Sentinel Rock in the estuary. When we were snorkelling in the rockpool we saw seven starfish and a leafy seadragon and I drew you one. You almost can't tell they're not seaweed. I think dad has sunstroke because he dressed in seaweed and danced in front of everyone. It was *so* embarrassing. A kid called James had sore feet and our friend made him sandals out of kelp!   bye for now, Penny

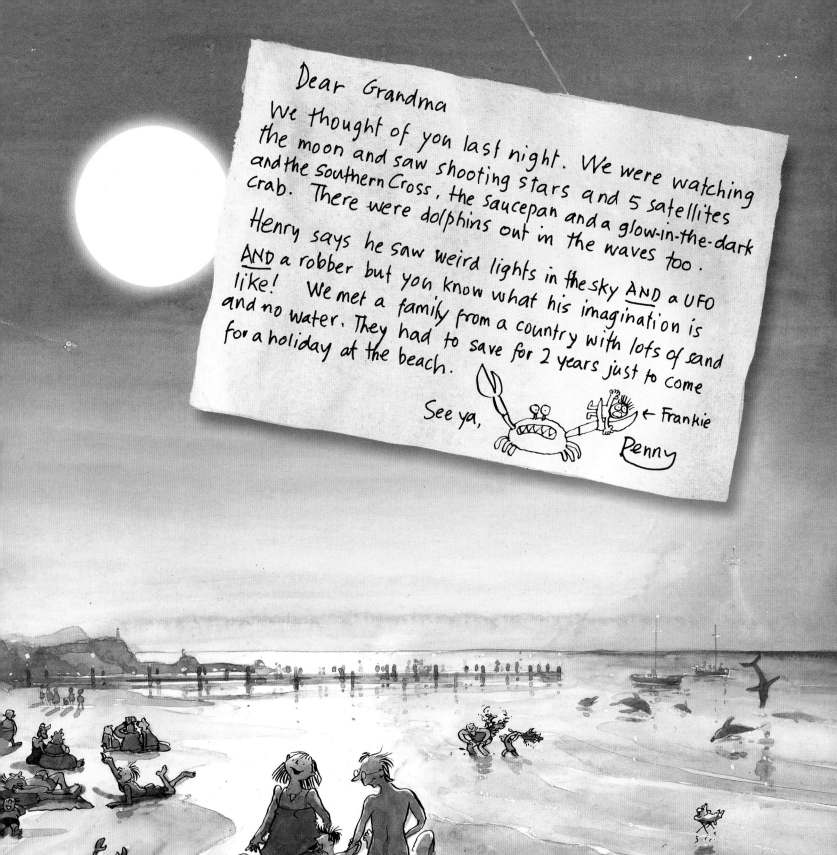

Dear Grandma

We thought of you last night. We were watching the moon and saw shooting stars and 5 satellites and the Southern Cross, the saucepan and a glow-in-the-dark crab. There were dolphins out in the waves too.

Henry says he saw weird lights in the sky AND a UFO AND a robber but you know what his imagination is like! We met a family from a country with lots of sand and no water. They had to save for 2 years just to come for a holiday at the beach.

See ya,

← Frankie

Penny

Dear Grandma, Today was the <u>BEST</u> day, we went diving again in the DEEP water and found SUNKEN TREASURE and SHIPWRECKS and a STINGRAY and an OCTOPUS and a GIANT CLAM!
I drew you a map so you can find the treasure if you come down to Crabby Spit. You will have to <u>be careful</u> because I think there will be things guarding it. And traps.
Good Luck. Love,

Henry

Cliffs
shallow
↗ To Crabby Spit
⊢ Deep water
sand
rock
X

Dear Grandma, We had a <u>real</u> adventure today! We hired bikes and rode all around Crabby Spit. Frankie said he saw a crocodile and I saw pelicans and swamphens and Hannah Colman. They were catching fish and eating them whole. YUCK!!!

And after lunch we went HORSERIDING and now dad won't sit down. He said his horse needed new springs. He was being the man from Snowy River and nearly fell into the water.

This is my invention. Do you think I'll get rich? xxxx Penny

I can't draw

spring seat

shocks!

roll-up ladder

Hey Grandma! We have been on a ferry today and smells like Henry's room because of all the bird poo. I don't think humans have ever been onto it! The sides are SO steep and there's just a little jetty.

On the pier we saw a man catch a squid. He was teasing it and it suddenly squirted a whole lot of black ink in his face! Serves him right. The man gave the squid to dad and I have a weird feeling dad thinks we're going to eat it. I'm having calamari from the shop, instead. I think I saw a giant octopus under the pier camouflaged as seaweed. Hope you're having fun too! My hair looks like this ➚

love, Penny

Dear Grandma, It is so NOT good it's our last Crabby Spit night!! We had a humungous bonfire on the beach and people got dressed up and sang and drummed and danced. We were HOT! ♡ Penny

Dear Grandma I have never seen such a big fire and we toasted marshmallows. I think even some of the grownups had a good time. It was so cool with the sea slooshing and the music jumping. I made up a dance and my head stayed still and my body danced around. My dad was being funny and he's done his back.
Love from Henry

DEAR GRANDMA I stayed up late and there was a very big fire. I found a crab. And there were dolphins swimming in the sea. LOVE. FRANKIE

First published in 2004

Copyright © Roland Harvey, 2004

Allen & Unwin
83 Alexander Street
Crows Nest NSW 2065
Australia
Phone: (61 2) 8425 0100
Fax: (61 2) 9906 2218
Email: info@allenandunwin.com
Web: www.allenandunwin.com

National Library of Australia
Cataloguing-in-Publication entry:

Harvey, Roland.
At the beach.

ISBN 1 74114 412 4.

I. Title.

A823.3

Illustration technique: dip pen and watercolour
Designed by Roland Harvey and Sandra Nobes
Printed in China by Everbest Printing Co.

5 7 9 10 8 6 4